Welcome to the darker sid of Halloween!

You braved the horrors of Halloween Horror Coloring Book Vol. 1...but now the shadows grow deeper. In Vol. 2, the nightmares have evolved into something darker and more sinister. Within these pages you'll encounter cursed relics, crumbling ruins, and creatures that lurk just beyond the candlelight. Are you ready to bring these haunted visions to life?

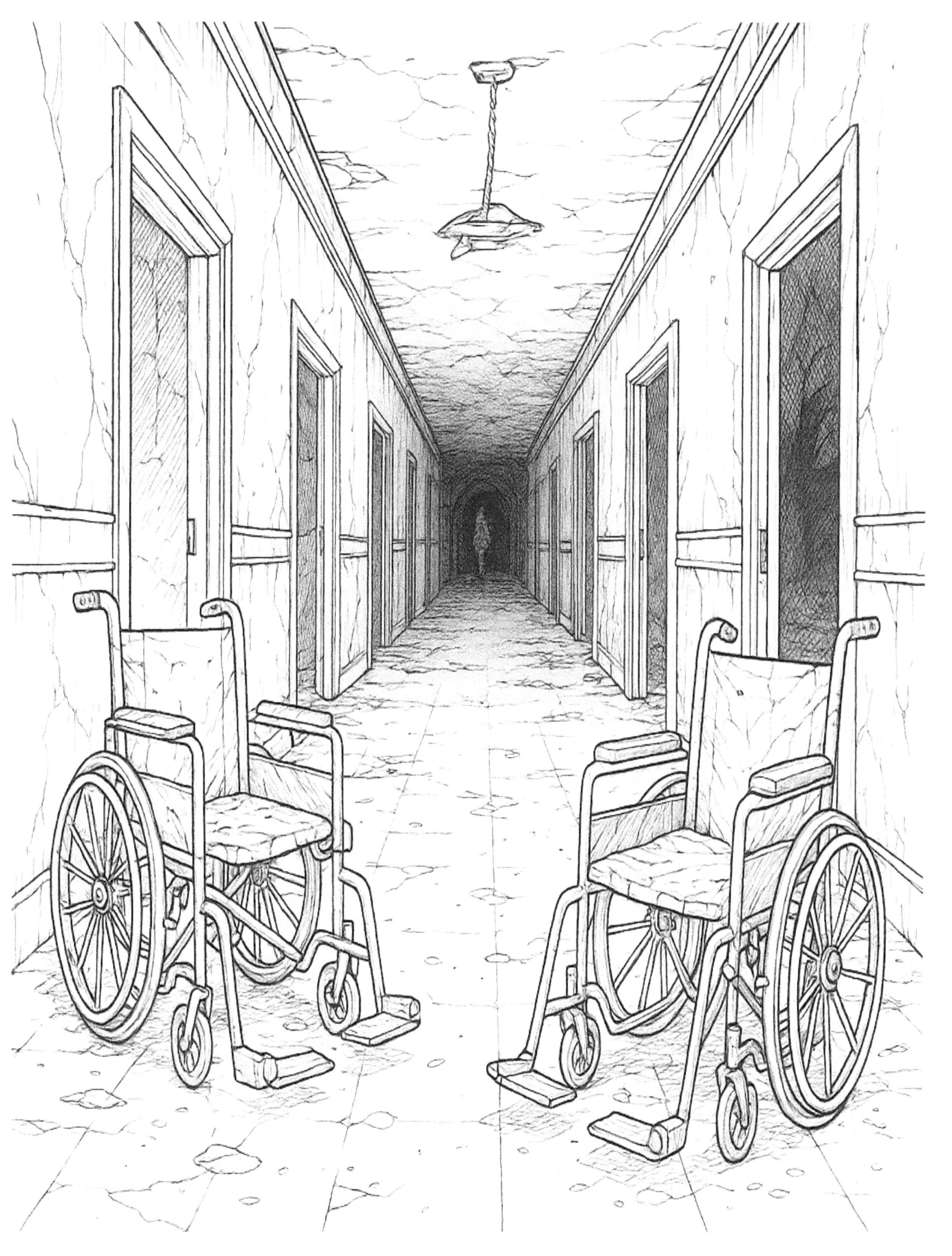

CARNIVAL

www.ingramcontent.com/pod-product-compliance
Lightning Source LLC
Chambersburg PA
CBHW041141300726
48978CB00016B/1346